THE STORY OF PAPER

BY

Ying Chang Compestine

ILLUSTRATED BY

YongSheng Xuan

Holiday House / New York

LONG AGO, BEFORE PAPER WAS INVENTED, most people in China
wrote on the ground with sticks or on their hands with slender brushes.
A few wealthy people wrote on silk.

At school students wrote using pointed sticks in the dirt. But the three
Kang boys, Ting, Pan, and Kùai, often found things on the ground that
were more interesting than their schoolwork.

"Ting and Pan, look at these big fat worms!" Kùai said.

"These ants are more interesting," Pan shouted.

"Look at this—," Ting began, but then the teacher came by.

"You three, over there." The teacher pointed to a place far away from the other students.

"Ten more math problems!"

"Ting and Pan, look—I'm using the worms to help me count," whispered Kùai.

"Grasshoppers are easier to add," Ting answered.

"But ants are easier to find," said Pan.

"Help—my grasshoppers are jumping away. I was adding six plus five. Now all I have is four plus three," Ting shouted, as he ran after his grasshoppers. When he returned, the rest of them had disappeared.

Once again the three boys didn't finish their work. Their teacher wrote a note to their parents on each boy's left hand, as he always did. "Be sure to hold up your hands and keep them dry," he ordered.

On Ting's hand he wrote, "Playing with grasshoppers."

On Pan's hand he wrote, "Playing with ants."

On Kùai's hand he wrote, "Playing with worms."

As the Kang boys passed the rice fields, the men working there called out, "Boys, what does the teacher say today?"

Ting lowered his hand and said, "Grasshoppers."

Pan hid his hand behind his back and said, "Ants."

Kùai covered his left hand with his right hand and said, "Worms."

"What does that mean?" The men looked at one another, puzzled. But the Kang boys had already run away.

As they passed the village well, the women who were washing clothes called out, "Boys, what does the teacher say today?"

Ting lowered his hand and said, "Grasshoppers."

Pan hid his hand behind his back and said, "Ants."

Kùai covered his left hand with his right hand and said, "Worms."

"What does that mean?" The women looked at one another, puzzled. But the Kang boys had already run away.

The three boys passed the old fruit tree in the village, where old women sewed and chatted, old men drank tea, and young children ate and played. The old women called out, "Boys, what does the teacher say today?"

Ting lowered his hand and said, "Grasshoppers."

Pan hid his hand behind his back and said, "Ants."

Kùai covered his left hand with his right hand and said, "Worms."

"What does that mean?" The old women looked at one another, puzzled. But the Kang boys had already run away.

When the Kang boys got home, they were all out of breath.

Ting gasped, "Why do people always want to know what the teacher said?"

"Because he is the smartest person in the village," Kùai answered, rubbing his left arm. "My arm is sore from holding up my hand all the way home."

"Mine too," Ting agreed. "I wish the teacher could write on something instead of our hands."

Kùai nodded in agreement. "Then the whole village wouldn't have to know about it."

"What else can he write on?" asked Pan. "We can't afford to write on silk and cloth like rich people in the city do."

"Mama makes clothes for rich people," said Kùai. "She has a basketful of scraps of silk and cloth–"

"But those tiny scraps are too small to write on," Pan interrupted.

"Perhaps we can make something out of those pieces," suggested Kùai.

"How?" asked Ting.

Papa and Mama Kang walked into the courtyard. "What's this we hear about ants, worms, and grasshoppers?" asked Mama.

"Were you boys playing on the ground again instead of doing your schoolwork?" Papa asked.

"What are we going to do with you boys?" Mama complained.

The three boys quickly lined up in front of Mama and Papa with their heads bowed.

"Those bugs like to play with us," said Kùai. "If only we could write on something besides the ground."

"Yes, those naughty bugs keep teasing us. I tried to add them up, but they jumped away," Ting added, standing behind Kùai.

Papa and Mama looked at each other and sighed.

"Now we have to make rice cakes. We'll talk about it after dinner," said Papa.

"I bet we won't have time to play again today," Pan whispered to his brothers.

"Let's hurry and pound the rice," said Kùai. "After we spread the mashed rice to dry, maybe Mama will let us play marbles."

Kùai used a wooden pestle to mash and beat the rice in a big wooden bucket. "This is easy," he said. "Mama has soaked the rice for two days, so it's soft and easy to mash."

Papa, Mama, and Pan carried three bamboo frames into the courtyard. Each frame held a large square of coarsely woven cloth.

"Can we pour the mashed rice now?" asked Kùai.

After peering into the bucket, Mama said, "Mash it twenty more times. I think that will be good enough."

Ting and Pan each mashed the rice ten more times. Kùai ran to get three big wooden bowls. Papa, Pan, Ting, and Mama set a bamboo frame on top of each bowl. They carefully poured the rice mixture onto each strainer. The water slowly drained through the fabric.

"The mashed rice should drain in half an hour. Then we'll steam it and make rice cakes," said Mama. She used a flat bamboo knife to smooth the surface of the mashed rice.

"Mama, can we play while the rice cakes drain?" asked Ting.

Mama looked at Papa and he nodded.

"Okay, but you all have to do more schoolwork after dinner," said Mama.

Ting and Pan ran to get their marbles. But Kùai stayed and stared for a long time at the smoothed surface of the mashed rice. A plan formed in his head.

The next day on the way to school Kùai told his brothers, "I have an idea for how to make something to write on."

"What? How?" asked Ting and Pan with great interest.

"Did you notice how smooth the surfaces of the rice cakes were yesterday? They were almost as smooth as the surface of silk," said Kùai.

"But you can't fold a rice cake. It's thick and sticky," said Ting, sounding disappointed.

"I don't want to write on a rice cake. I want to eat it!" Pan smacked his lips.

"What if we use something other than rice?" asked Kùai. He told his brothers his plan.

That night after Mama and Papa fell asleep, the three boys quietly went into action. Kùai dumped the big basket of Mama's small pieces of silk and other cloth into the wooden bucket. Pan poured in a big bucket of water to soak the fabric.

"What about adding some bark and twigs?" Ting asked. "It will give it a good flavor."

"Why not?" Kùai threw two handfuls of twigs and bark into the bucket.

"I bet some wood slivers and leaves will give this stew a delicious taste, too," exclaimed Pan, throwing in a handful of leaves and wood slivers.

Ting and Pan started to giggle. Kùai quickly covered their mouths with his hands. "Shhh...be quiet! You'll wake up Mama and Papa."

Together they hid the bucket under some big leaves.

Two days later, when Mama and Papa were out, the three boys pulled out their invention.

"Ting, make sure you beat and mash all the fabric," said Kùai.

They took turns beating and mashing the mixture into a pulp.

"My arm hurts," complained Ting. "I think the mash is ready for the next step."

"How about if we each mash it twenty more times? If this works, the teacher will have something to write on. Then the whole village will never know what the teacher said about us," Kùai said with a big laugh.

When Mama and Papa came home, they were surprised to see all the bamboo rice cake strainers, the dinner table, the rest of the furniture, and even the walls of the courtyard covered with thin sheets of something that looked like cloth, but wasn't.

Mama cried, "What happened here?"

The three boys were standing in line in front of a wall. Kùai was writing on a thin sheet pressed against the wall. Ting was using Kùai's back as a table, writing on another thin sheet. And Pan was writing on yet another thin sheet on Ting's back.

After the boys explained their invention to Papa and Mama, the Kang family decided to present these thin sheets to the teacher.

The next day at school the teacher wrote his first note to Mama and Papa using one of the sheets. He wrote, "I am going to present the boys' invention to the emperor." The teacher carefully folded the sheet and handed it to Kùai.

"Today, nobody will know what the teacher wrote except us," said Ting.

"But I want everybody to know about our invention," said Kùai as he slowly unfolded the teacher's note.

"Me too, me too," agreed Ting and Pan.

The three boys took turns carrying the teacher's note above their heads, as they slowly walked through the village with big smiles on their faces.

One by one, all the villagers, young and old, followed the boys. The villagers looked at the teacher's note. They talked about how wonderful it was to have an invention from their village to present to the emperor. They talked about how smart the Kang boys were....

The emperor thought the boys' invention was a great idea and named the thin sheets *zhi*—paper.

As for the Kang family, they opened the world's very first paper factory. The Kang boys seldom got into trouble at school because they no longer had to do their work on the ground. Now they had more time to play with grasshoppers, ants, and worms at home.

AUTHOR'S NOTE

Paper originated in China. The oldest pieces of paper that still exist were found in a Chinese tomb built at the beginning of the Han dynasty (206 B.C.E. to 220 C.E.).

Before the invention of paper, the Chinese people wrote on pieces of bone, turtle shell, and bamboo. Writing on these materials required a great amount of time and effort.

Silk and other cloths were also used for writing and were made into books. As these were expensive, they could only be used by the wealthy and were out of reach of the common people. Many narrow strips of extra fabric were trimmed away in the process of making books. Finding a way to use this wasted material inspired the invention of paper.

Small pieces of the wasted cloth were first soaked in water and then beaten with a pestle by hand until reduced to fiber. This pulp was spread on screenlike mats from which the water drained, leaving the interwoven fibers to form thin sheets. The two old Chinese characters for *paper* combine the words for both silk and cloth.

Ts'si Lun, who worked as a court official, conceived of the idea of adding other raw material to the paper mixture. This included old fishnets, bark, twigs, wood slivers, hemp waste, and old rags. In 105 C.E. Ts'si Lun officially reported the invention of paper to the emperor.

The emperor gave Ts'si Lun a large reward and made papermaking an official task. Later, methods of papermaking spread to other countries, including the United States.

HOMEMADE GARDEN PAPER

This simple recipe will make two 3-inch round pieces of colorful paper.
Be creative! You can replace the rose petals and leaves with other garden plants,
even vegetables. You can also add a few drops of food coloring. To make larger
paper, double or triple the recipe and use a container with a wider opening.

You will need:

a 2-foot length of toilet paper, torn into small pieces
$1\frac{1}{4}$ cups water
6 small rose petals
6 small rose leaves
1 wide-mouthed mason jar or large glass with a 3-inch-wide mouth
2 sheets of cheesecloth, cut into 8-by-8-inch squares
1 thick rubber band
1 towel

With the help of an adult, combine the paper, water, rose petals, and rose leaves
in a blender. Blend until the mixture becomes pulp, about 1 minute.

Pour half the pulp into the jar. Place the cheesecloth over the mouth of the jar
and fasten it in place with the thick rubber band. Turn the jar upside down over
a sink. Gently shake the jar and pat the cheesecloth until all the water drains out.

Keeping the jar upside down, place it on the towel. Unfasten the rubber band.
Lift away the jar. Fold the cheesecloth over the pulp. Fold the towel over the
cheesecloth. Press out any remaining water with your hands. To finish drying
the paper, set it in the sun or in a warm oven. Repeat with the remaining pulp.

To my two creative papermakers,
Greg and Vinson
Y. C. C.

To my friend Wang Yao
and the Zhao Jing Fu family
Y. X.

Library of Congress Cataloging-in-Publication Data

Compestine, Ying Chang.
The story of paper / by Ying Chang Compestine;
illustrated by YongSheng Xuan.–1st ed.
p. cm.
Summary: After the Kang brothers get in trouble at school, they devise a way to make paper,
which will make things easier for both their teacher and themselves.
Includes a historical note and a recipe for home-made paper.

ISBN 0-8234-1705-0 (hardcover)

[1. Papermaking—Fiction. 2. Schools—Fiction. 3. China—History—Fiction.]
I. Xuan, YongSheng, ill. II. Title.
PZ7.C73615St 2003
[E]—dc21
2002191317